This book belongs to

Hidden in the broom cupboard of
Rose Cottage is the most delightful little
house. Shh, it's a secret. No one knows
it's there . . . This is the home of
Tumtum and Nutmeg . . .

When Arthur and Lucy are sent to
stay with their Uncle Jeremy at the
seaside, Tumtum and Nutmeg
decide to go along and keep an eye
on them. But then the mice stumble
upon an abandoned doll's house and
a mysterious treasure map – and all
sorts of adventures unfold!

Also by Emily Bearn

A SEASIDE ADVENTURE

by Emily Bearn

Illustrated by Nick Price

EGMONT

EGMONT

We bring stories to life

A Seaside Adventure
First published 2010
by Egmont UK Limited
239 Kensington High Street, London W8 6SA

Text copyright © 2010 Emily Bearn
Cover and inside illustrations copyright © 2010 Nick Price

The moral rights of the author and illustrator have been asserted

ISBN 978 1 4052 4820 4

1 3 5 7 9 10 8 6 4 2

www.egmont.co.uk

A CIP catalogue record for this title is available
from the British Library

Typeset by Avon DataSet Ltd, Bidford on Avon, Warwickshire
Printed and bound in Italy by L.E.G.O.S.P.A

For Mark

Chapter One

Tumtum was sitting at the kitchen table, with his head slumped in his paws. '*The seaside?* But we can't possibly go to the seaside,' he groaned. 'We might be chased by a crab!'

Tumtum had heard very frightening things about the seaside. He didn't like the sound of it at all.

But Nutmeg's mind was already made up. 'If Arthur and Lucy are going to the seaside, then we are going too,' she said firmly.

'When are they leaving?' Tumtum asked miserably.

'Tomorrow morning,' Nutmeg replied. 'I must say, I wish they'd given us a little more warning!'

She had only learned of the trip a few minutes ago, when she had poked her head into the kitchen and heard the children discussing it.

'They're going to stay with their Uncle Jeremy,' she went on. 'And would you believe it, Mr Mildew is going to let them travel by train *all on their own*! We shall have to stow away in one of their rucksacks and keep an eye on them.'

Tumtum scowled. The last time he'd stowed away in a rucksack it had been very uncomfortable.

'How long are they going for?' he asked.

'A week,' Nutmeg replied.

'*A week!*' Tumtum cried. A week is a long time in a mouse's life. 'Who will look after Nutmouse Hall?' he asked.

'I shall ask Mrs Marchmouse to come and keep an eye on things,' Nutmeg said busily. 'Now don't look so glum, dear. The sea air will do us good. And a week will go by in a flash. You shall love it once you're there!'

'No I shan't!' Tumtum muttered. The very thought of the seaside made him shudder. He knew he wouldn't like it one bit.

'I hope this doesn't turn into another adventure,' he said glumly.

'Of course it won't, dear,' Nutmeg replied.

But Tumtum wasn't so sure.

The following day, towards teatime, there was a sudden *Toot! Toot!* then a loud clatter of brakes, as the express train drew into Mousewall-on-Sea.

'Hooray! We're here!' Arthur shouted, leaping from his seat. They had been cooped up in the train carriage for hours, and he was longing to get out.

Lucy sat up, looking a little startled. She had been asleep, and her toes were full of pins and needles.

'Can you see him?' Arthur asked, pulling down their bags from the luggage rack.

Lucy pressed her nose to the window, and peered into the throng of faces on the platform.

'There he is!' she cried.

She had only met Uncle Jeremy once before, and that had been ages ago, when she was only seven. But she spotted him at once, for he looked quite different to anyone else. He was round and comfortable, with a red nose, and a waistcoat stretched so tightly over his stomach that the buttons looked as if they were about to go *Ping!*

'Here's your bag,' Arthur said, heaving down Lucy's rucksack. 'Crikey! What did you pack in it? It weighs a ton!'

'Well at least I didn't bring four pairs of shoes like you did,' Lucy replied.

But Arthur was right — when she pulled her rucksack on to her back it did feel rather heavy. It was curious, for she was sure she hadn't packed much.

But as soon as they got off the train she forgot

all about it, because there was so much else to think about.

The children had never been to Mousewall before, and it all felt very strange. Uncle Jeremy drove them home through a maze of little wriggling lanes, with hedges so high you couldn't see over them.

Then finally they came to the top of a very tall hill – and when they looked down, they could see the sea, spread out like a big sheet of silver.

Uncle Jeremy stopped the car a moment so they could have a look.

In front of them was a thin road, twisting down to a crescent-shaped bay circled by green cliffs. In the middle of the bay there was a little beach, and a cluster of cottages.

'That would be a nice place to live,' Arthur said enviously.

'Well, I'm glad you think so,' Uncle Jeremy replied.

'Is that where *you* live?' the children cried. 'Oh, how wonderful!'

Uncle Jeremy looked very pleased. Then he started the car again, and drove all the way down the hill, until they came to a white cottage with fishing nets piled in front of it, and a sign saying

on the door.

The children piled out of the car and looked around in delight. The cottage was on a narrow lane, and just on the other side of the lane was a tall

stone wall, with steps leading down to the beach. They had known that Uncle Jeremy's house was by the sea – but they hadn't expected it to be as close as this.

And Smugglers' Keep was such a mysterious name for a cottage, they felt something exciting was sure to happen to them there.

'Come in and I'll show you your room,' Uncle Jeremy said, hauling their bags out of the car. He opened the front door, and the children ran inside to explore.

Smugglers' Keep was very old. The furniture was dark and dusty, and the floorboards creaked. The children's bedroom was at the top of the house, and it had tall wooden beds and a pointed window looking out to sea.

'Well, you sort yourselves out, then we can have supper,' Uncle Jeremy said, dropping their bags on the floor. 'Mrs Blythe's made a fish pie.'

Uncle Jeremy had already told the children about Mrs Blythe. She was his housekeeper, and she did everything for him – or at least everything that Uncle Jeremy felt he couldn't do himself, such as cooking and cleaning, and making beds.

'We'll be down in a minute,' Arthur said. He hadn't eaten anything since lunch, and his stomach was rumbling.

'I'll have this bed,' he said, claiming the one nearest the window.

'All right,' Lucy said, thinking it wasn't worth arguing about. She tossed her rucksack on to the other bed, nearest the door – and as it landed, she heard something squeak. 'Goodness, doesn't this room feel funny,' she said. 'Everything creaks!'

Arthur ran to open the window, and that creaked too.

Then – 'Wow!' Lucy said. 'Look at that!' For tucked beside the wardrobe was a big doll's house, with pale pink walls and peppermint shutters. Lucy thought it was the prettiest doll's house she had ever seen. And yet when she peeked inside it was quite empty. There was not a stick of furniture, not even a bed. 'I wonder whose it is,' she said. 'It's odd that it doesn't have anything in it.'

'Oh, I don't know. Maybe it belonged to Uncle Jeremy when he was a little boy,' Arthur said. He wasn't interested in doll's houses. He wanted to explore the beach.

But Lucy thought it was rather mysterious. 'If only we were here longer, I could make some furniture for it,' she said. She was still gazing at it as she pulled open the strings of her rucksack, and started tugging the contents out on to the bed.

'Oh, come on,' Arthur said impatiently. 'We can unpack later. Let's have tea first.'

'Hang on. It won't take long,' Lucy said.

'But I'm starving!' Arthur groaned, hovering at the doorway.

'Oh, all right,' Lucy sighed. Then she dropped the rucksack back on her bed, and ran after him downstairs. And it was just as well she didn't finish unpacking, or she would have found something most unexpected hidden among her clothes.

Chapter Two

Tumtum and Nutmeg clambered out of Lucy's rucksack on to the bed, pulling their luggage behind them.

And what a lot of luggage there was!

Four suitcases, two deckchairs, a folding table, a windbreak, a swimming bag, Tumtum's fishing net, Nutmeg's sewing basket and two picnic hampers – one for savouries, and one for sweets.

No wonder Lucy's rucksack felt heavy!

The Nutmouses were very stiff. They had been travelling all day long, squashed up inside one of Lucy's slippers.

'I'm aching all over,' Tumtum groaned.

Nutmeg was aching too. But once they had stretched their legs on the bed they began to feel better.

'Come on, we'd better find somewhere to hide before the children come back from supper,' Nutmeg said.

They stood gazing around the room, searching for a suitable hideaway.

'What about that doll's house!' Nutmeg exclaimed. 'Doesn't it look grand! It would make a splendid holiday home!' The windows had been left open, and she could see inside the rooms: 'We wouldn't be getting in anyone's way – it looks quite abandoned,' she said. 'It's not even furnished!'

Tumtum shook his head. 'It would be much too obvious – Lucy's sure to look inside it, and imagine what a fright she'll get if she finds that we've moved in. Let's try under there,' he suggested, pointing to a big chest of drawers in the corner. It was raised on four legs, so there would be just enough room for them to stand up underneath.

'We'll be well hidden – the children will never see us,' he said.

Nutmeg agreed, and that was how the adventure began.

They dropped all their luggage over the edge of the bed, then they climbed down the blankets, and dragged everything under the chest of drawers.

But it was not at all agreeable. It was dark and gloomy, and the floor was covered in cobwebs.

'Surely we could find a nicer hiding place than this,' Nutmeg said, scrunching her nose. 'Why don't we try inside one of the bedside tables?'

Tumtum shook his head. 'If we camp in a bedside table, the children will be sure to find us,' he said. 'This is much safer. And once we've set up our picnic table it will look more homely.'

He dug out the camping light, so they could see what they were doing. But when he shone it round, they both stared in surprise. For in the wall behind them there was a little round mouse-hole, with a green door and a shiny brass bell. And beside the door was a sign saying:

LORD SEAMOUSE OF
SEAVIEW HOLLOW

'Gracious!' they exclaimed. They hadn't expected to find another mouse living here.

'Perhaps we'd better go and hide somewhere else,' Nutmeg said anxiously – for Lord Seamouse sounded rather a frightening name.

'Don't be silly, dear,' Tumtum replied. 'Now we're here, we must ring the bell.'

'Oh, please don't!' Nutmeg cried – but before they could decide whether to ring it or not to ring it, the door opened and a fat white mouse in a green waistcoat appeared. This was Lord Seamouse and, goodness, he did look lordly! He was wearing a

LORD SEAMOUSE OF SEAVIEW HOLLOW

watch on a gold chain, and a pair of satin slippers.

Lord Seamouse hadn't seen another mouse for weeks, so he was rather startled. 'Are you here to collect the rent?' he asked anxiously.

'No, no, nothing like that,' Tumtum reassured him. 'We're here to look after Arthur and Lucy.'

Lord Seamouse looked very baffled – for, of course, he had never heard of Arthur and Lucy. So when the Nutmouses had introduced themselves, they had to tell him the whole story – about how they were the children's secret guardians, and how they had travelled all the way from Rose Cottage in the bottom of Lucy's rucksack.

Lord Seamouse nodded, and looked very impressed.

'So we hope you won't mind if we camp

under your chest of drawers for a few days,' Nutmeg said finally.

'You shall do no such thing!' Lord Seamouse said in a booming voice. 'You shall both stay in Seaview Hollow with me! Now come on in. You're just in time for tea!'

Tumtum and Nutmeg looked delighted.

Lord Seamouse helped them drag everything inside. He was astonished by how much luggage they had. But when he saw Tumtum's family crest on the suitcases, he supposed they must be rather grand.

When the last case had been dragged in, Lord Seamouse gave them a tour of his mouse-hole. It wasn't at all like the sort of mouse-hole you would expect a Lord to live in. The rooms were small and poky, and the furniture was all hotchpotch. The beds were made out of matchboxes, and the dining-room table was a yogurt pot.

When he had shown them round, Lord Seamouse laid a trolley with tea and ginger cake, and scones with clotted cream and jam on top. Then they all sat down beside the drawing-room fire, in armchairs made out of seashells.

'Have you always lived here?' Nutmeg began.

'In this hollow! Oh, gracious no!' Lord Seamouse spluttered. 'In fact, it's rather a long story –'

And he was about to tell it, but then all of a sudden the doorbell rang.

Lord Seamouse jumped.

'Two sets of visitors in one afternoon!' he said in astonishment. This really was unusual. He hurried through to the hall, wondering who it could be.

The Nutmouses waited by the fire. Presently they heard footsteps in the hall, and a voice which sounded oddly familiar. And when Lord Seamouse showed the new arrival into the drawing room, they could hardly believe their eyes!

'Well blow me!' Tumtum stammered. 'If it isn't General Marchmouse!'

Chapter Three

The Nutmouses were astonished. They had seen the General yesterday, and told him about their trip. But he hadn't mentioned anything about coming too.

'How did you get here?' Tumtum asked.

'In the same rucksack as you!' the General replied shiftily. 'I was hiding in Lucy's sponge bag. I crept on board last night. I've never been to the seaside, so when I heard you were going, I decided to come too!'

'Does Mrs Marchmouse know you're here?' Nutmeg asked. Poor Mrs Marchmouse. The General was always running away from home, and it made her terribly fussed.

'She'll know by now,' the General said, looking a little guilty. 'I left her a note on the breakfast table.'

Tumtum and Nutmeg sighed. They should have known better than to tell the General about their trip – for he could never resist an adventure. And whenever he turned up, trouble seemed to follow. Which is why the Nutmouses were not altogether pleased to see him.

But Lord Seamouse didn't know how

troublesome the General could be. He was delighted to have another visitor. 'I shall go and make some more tea,' he said. 'And I believe I've some jam tarts left, unless that nuisance of a cockroach has eaten them all.'

Lord Seamouse hurried off to the kitchen. But as he reappeared, there was a huge crash which made the whole mouse-hole tremor. The paintings shook on the walls, and the cups rattled in their saucers.

'Help!' Lord Seamouse cried, ducking behind the trolley.

'There's no need to worry, it's only the children coming back,' Nutmeg said calmly.

The children crashed and banged all the time in Rose Cottage, so she and Tumtum were quite used to it by now.

But Lord Seamouse looked horrified. There hadn't been any children at Smugglers' Keep in his lifetime, so he didn't know how noisy they could be.

'They won't give you any trouble,' Nutmeg assured him. 'And if the weather's fine they'll spend most of their time outdoors.'

Lord Seamouse sat down in his seashell, feeling rather shaken.

'What do human children *do*?' he asked curiously.

'Oh, lots of things,' Tumtum replied. 'They play football and cricket and hide-and-seek, and they bake cakes and they make model aeroplanes, and they read books –'

'*They can read?*' Lord Seamouse asked in astonishment.

'Oh, yes,' Nutmeg replied. 'And they can write too!'

Lord Seamouse stroked his whiskers. He looked deep in thought.

'Do you think they could read a map?' he asked eventually.

'Of course,' Tumtum said. 'They are a highly intelligent breed.'

'Then they might be just what I need!' Lord Seamouse said excitedly.

'How do you mean?' Nutmeg asked.

Lord Seamouse got up, and walked over to his desk. He opened the drawer, and took out a brown envelope labelled:

Then he pulled a piece of crumpled paper from it, and passed it round so everyone could see.

'It's a map!' the General exclaimed. He always loved a good map to read. And this one looked very intriguing.

It showed a beach covered in sandcastles, with a line of big craggy rocks down one side. The biggest rock had its name written beside it – Stargazer – and it was marked with a silver cross.

'What does it all mean?' he asked excitedly.

'It is a treasure map!' Lord Seamouse said in a hushed tone. He leaned over, and traced it with his paw. 'The beach is just here, in front of the cottage. And the cross marks where the treasure is hidden – in a cave inside Stargazer Rock!'

'What treasure?' the General asked.

'Why, my treasure of course!' Lord Seamouse replied. 'The Lost Treasures of Seaview Manor!'

'Seaview Manor?' everyone asked, looking very confused.

'Yes, Seaview Manor,' Lord Seamouse said impatiently. 'You must have noticed it when you were travelling across the bedroom floor. It's the finest manor house in all of Mousewall!'

'Oh, you mean the doll's house!' Nutmeg said. 'Yes, we did admire it. But it looked abandoned. Does no one live there?'

Lord Seamouse sighed. He could see that he

would have to explain everything from the very beginning.

'The last person to live in Seaview Manor was me!' he said. 'And, oh, you should have seen the house then! I lived just as a Lord should. There were tapestries and chandeliers and four-poster beds . . . and a piano and a ping-pong table . . . and the drawing-room chairs were upholstered in chintz! Every room was appointed to the highest standard. And if you could only have seen the dinners I hosted in the dining room! Do you know, my dears – the table could seat twelve!'

Lord Seamouse wiped a tear from his eye. Thinking about his old home always made him cry.

'Whose doll's house was it?' the General asked.

'It had belonged to Uncle Jeremy when he was a little boy,' Lord Seamouse said. 'He used to keep it downstairs in the drawing room. But it got in the way rather – so one day he dumped it up here. And that's when I moved in!'

'Did Uncle Jeremy never see you?' Nutmeg asked.

'Oh, no,' Lord Seamouse replied. 'Uncle Jeremy seldom comes up here. And besides, he's much too old to be playing with doll's houses now.'

'So what happened to all the furniture?' Tumtum wondered. It was clear Lord Seamouse hadn't brought any of it to Seaview Hollow. Everything here was very shabby.

'It was stolen – every last stick!' Lord

Seamouse said. 'I went out for a stroll one day, and when I came home, Seaview Manor had been stripped bare. They took everything – the wardrobes, the beds, the fish knives – they even took my stuffed beetles!'

'Who?' everyone cried.

'Beach mice,' Lord Seamouse said distastefully. 'Rum sorts, who sleep rough in sandcastles – Mousewall's full of them. Anyway, word had gone round that I had a lot of fancy things, and one day a gang of them came up here and stole the whole lot. My cleaning mouse, old Mrs Moptail, was polishing the silver when they arrived, and they tied her up! When I got home, she was the only thing left!'

Everyone looked very shocked.

'What a terrible story,' Nutmeg said.

'Yes, it was rather,' Lord Seamouse replied. 'Mrs Moptail was in a dreadful state. And I couldn't even make her a cup of tea – because the rotters had taken my kettle! Well, I couldn't stay in Seaview Manor without any furniture. It felt much too bleak. So I moved in here, to Seaview Hollow. And of course it's perfectly cosy and all that . . . But . . . well, it's not quite the same.'

The others nodded in sympathy. They could see why the Hollow must seem rather a come down after life at the Manor.

'Was Uncle Jeremy upset when everything disappeared?' Nutmeg asked.

'Oh, he never bothers with the doll's house. He hasn't even noticed the furniture's gone,' Lord Seamouse replied. 'But of course the thieves took his teeth too!'

'*His teeth?!*' everyone cried.

'Yes, his teeth,' Lord Seamouse said. 'All his milk teeth – you know, the ones that fell out when he was a boy. I found them in Seaview Manor soon after I moved in. They were hidden under a bed!'

'Were there many?' Tumtum asked.

'Oh, yes. A full set!' Lord Seamouse replied proudly.

Everyone gasped, for human teeth are very valuable things. If a wicked mouse creeps up in the night and plucks one from under a child's pillow, he can trade it with the tooth fairies for a gold coin. So just think how much a whole set would be worth!

'How did they end up under the bed?' Tumtum asked.

'One of the tooth fairies must have hidden them there when Uncle Jeremy was a little boy,' Lord Seamouse replied. 'Each time she collected another tooth from under Uncle Jeremy's pillow, she would have added it to the pile, until eventually there was a full set. They were very dusty when I found them. You could tell no one had touched them for years.'

'But why would the tooth fairy have left them there so long?' Nutmeg asked.

'Oh, you know what fairies are like,' Lord Seamouse said snootily. 'Very silly creatures — always forgetting things. The poor fairy probably couldn't remember where she'd hidden them!'

'What did you do with them?' Nutmeg asked.

'I polished them up, and displayed them in my drawing-room cabinet,' Lord Seamouse replied. 'All my visitors admired them – and they became rather a talking point. That was my mistake, of course. Because soon every mouse in the village seemed to know that there was a full set of milk teeth in Seaview Manor – so I suppose it's hardly surprising I was robbed.'

'Couldn't you catch the thieves?' Tumtum asked.

'Oh, we tried,' Lord Seamouse said. 'Every police mouse in Mousewall was on The Case of The Missing Teeth. And our local *Mouse Gazette* ran a big story on it – there was even a reward on their heads. But the rascals were very clever. They didn't leave a single clue.'

'So, what about this map?' the General asked impatiently.

'That's the exciting part,' Lord Seamouse said. 'The other day, the post mouse arrived here with a letter. And to my surprise, it was from one of the thieves himself – a fellow called Black Jaw. And very strange it was too. He said he was the only one of his gang left. The rest of them came to a sticky end, or so he told me. Apparently they were stealing sweets from the village shop, and they got trapped in a jar of sherbet!'

'Ooh! How horrid,' Nutmeg said.

'What happened to Black Jaw?' Tumtum asked.

'He got away,' Lord Seamouse said. 'And without the others to egg him on, he began to mend his ways. He stopped thieving, and started cleaning mouse-holes for a living. But he didn't get much work, because all the mice around these parts knew him for a crook. So he decided to move on up the coast, and start his life all over again.

'But he felt so bad about robbing Seaview Manor that before he went he sent me this map, showing me where the gang had hidden everything they stole. And he said that the teeth are still there too.'

'How thrilling,' the General cried. 'Then we must go at once, and get everything back!'

'Oh, that would be out of the question,' Lord Seamouse said. 'Stargazer's the tallest rock on the whole beach – as tall as two grown men! If you stand in front of it, you can see it's full of caves.

The treasure is hidden in one of them, but the rock face is much too steep to climb.'

'Then how did Black Jaw's gang get there?' Tumtum asked.

'They went up the Secret Tunnel inside the rock,' Lord Seamouse replied. 'But the tunnel begins in the Grotto. And to reach the Grotto you have to cross the Rock Pool. And if you try to cross the Rock Pool, you'll be gobbled alive by the Crabby Crab! Well, Black Jaw's gang had a big boat, so they could get past him all right. But I've only a lilo, so I'd never survive!'

Nutmeg turned pale. She didn't like the sound of the Crabby Crab one bit. But the General was fearless: 'Bother your silly crab! I shall find the cave!' he cried.

Lord Seamouse laughed. 'I wouldn't try it, old boy – you'll come to a sticky end!'

The General scowled. He didn't like being laughed at. 'Well, if you don't let me try, then you'll never get your treasure back,' he said grumpily.

'Oh, but I will – now that these two human children have appeared!' Lord Seamouse beamed. 'Don't you see? *They* can climb up the rock and dig the treasure out. It would be no trouble for those giants. They could carry the entire contents of Seaview Manor home in a pillow case!'

Lord Seamouse's face shone. At long last, he might see all his lovely things again.

Nutmeg looked anxious. 'Are you sure they wouldn't come to harm?'

'Of course not,' Lord Seamouse replied. 'The

rock wouldn't seem very big to them. And the Crabby Crab won't give them any trouble – it will flee to the bottom of the pool when it sees two humans coming!'

'I think it's a capital plan,' Tumtum said. 'Just think how thrilled they'll be!'

Nutmeg agreed – the children would love a treasure hunt. 'I'll leave the map on Lucy's bedside table tonight, and I'll write them a letter, explaining exactly what to do,' she said.

Lord Seamouse hurried to his desk, and found her a piece of paper.

Everyone was very excited. But General Marchmouse had suddenly become quiet. Crabby Crabs! Caves! Secret Tunnels! Why, this was just the sort of adventure he craved. And he didn't see why

Arthur and Lucy should have all the fun. He shot a sideways glance at the map, which Lord Seamouse had left on his chair. *Bother the children*, the General thought slyly. *I'll find the cave first! And I'll bring back the teeth! And, oh, just think what a hero I shall be!*

Chapter Four

Later that evening, when the children were asleep, Tumtum and Nutmeg crept out to leave the map on Lucy's bedside table.

When they got back to Seaview Hollow, Lord Seamouse made some cocoa. Then they sat up talking in the drawing room. But General Marchmouse didn't say much. He had decided that as soon as the others had gone to bed, he would sneak out and steal the map back! Then he would set off for the beach at dawn, and find the treasure all by himself!

He fidgeted in his armchair, wishing they would all turn in. But on and on they chattered. The General found their talk very dull. His long day had tired him. He became drowsier and drowsier, and his eyelids felt like lead.

By the time Nutmeg offered him another mug of cocoa, he was fast asleep.

She gave him a prod, but he didn't stir.

'We might as well let him sleep here. There's no point moving him,' Lord Seamouse said.

Tumtum pulled off his shoes, and Nutmeg tucked a warm blanket round him. Then they all went off to bed, leaving the General snoring in his armchair.

When the General woke up in the morning he felt very foggy. He heard the clock chime seven, and he rubbed his eyes, trying to remember what he was supposed to do.

Then he gave a gulp. '*THE MAP!*' he cried.

He threw off his blanket, and sprang from the chair. Then he let himself out of the mouse-hole, and crept into the children's room.

But when he peeked out from under the chest of drawers he let out a howl. He was too late! Arthur and Lucy were already awake. They had found the map, and Nutmeg's letter. And now they were sitting poring over them on Lucy's bed.

The General seethed. If only he hadn't fallen asleep!

Lucy was reading the letter through the

magnifying glass attached to Arthur's pen knife.

'Oh, hurry! What does it say?' Arthur said impatiently.

Lucy held it up to her face, and read it out loud:

Dear Arthur and Lucy,

You will have noticed that there is a big doll's house in your bedroom — but you would never guess what a mysterious tale it has to tell. For it isn't really a doll's house. It is the home of a Very Important Creature called Lord Seamouse. But one day, all Lord Seamouse's beautiful treasures were stolen by a gang of thieves. He was quite heartbroken — and since he no longer had a bed to sleep on, he had to move out.

But now, my dears, you might be able to help.
Attached to this letter you will find a map of the
beach in front of Smugglers' Keep. Be sure to take
good care of it, for this map is very special. It is a
Treasure Map, showing where all the treasures from
the doll's house are hidden. If you follow the map,
you will be able to find them, and put everything
back in place.
Love,
Nutmeg.
P.S. Say nothing of this to Uncle Jeremy. We don't
want any grown-ups interfering in our adventure.

The children were astonished.

'What sort of creature do you think Lord
Seamouse is?' Lucy asked.

'I don't know,' Arthur said. 'And if he's half as secretive as Nutmeg, then we shan't be seeing much of him!'

Lucy frowned. It was true. Nutmeg never appeared. But she was longing to know more about this mysterious-sounding Lord. 'With a name like that, maybe he's a mouse,' she said.

'Don't be silly,' Arthur said. 'Mice don't have titles. Now come on! Let's hurry up and find this treasure!'

They quickly got dressed and had breakfast, then they set out.

'Stay in front of the house, where I can see you, and don't go climbing any rocks,' Mrs Blythe fussed.

'We won't,' they replied, hurtling out of the

front door.

They crossed the lane, and ran down the steps to the beach. It was a very small beach, about the size of a tennis court, and this morning there was no one else there. There were just some rowing boats propped against the wall, and three canoes lying upside down in the sand.

On one side of the beach there was a little harbour full of fishing boats. And on the other side there was a line of tall black rocks, snaking down to the sea.

The children shaded their eyes, for it was already hot, and the sun was making the sand glare.

Arthur pulled out the map, and then they tried to work out what was what. But the drawing was so small that the lines just looked like squiggles.

Lucy had to have a long look through the magnifying glass before she could make any sense of it.

'I've got it!' she said finally. Then she held the map so Arthur could see, and pointed each thing out:

'There's the sea . . . and that's the harbour wall . . . and these shapes must be those big rocks over there. And the cross is on the biggest rock. So that must be where the treasure's hidden! Come on! We'll find it in no time!'

'Hang on,' Arthur said. 'What are these?' He was pointing to some tiny marks on the side of the map, beside where the cross was drawn.

Lucy peered through the magnifying glass again. The marks were so small, that at first they just looked like dots and dashes. But when she looked harder, she could see that they were letters.

She studied each one very carefully, and read them aloud . . . 'S – T – A – R . . . Stargazer!' she said. 'That must be the name of the rock where the treasure's hidden!'

Stargazer. It sounded very mysterious.

'Come on. Let's go and find it!' Arthur said.

They ran over to the rocks, and stood looking at them from the sand. In the front, the rocks were smooth and flat, like giant pebbles. But the rocks behind were much bigger. Some were as tall as a front door.

'That must be Stargazer,' Arthur said, pointing to the tallest rock of all.

It was very different to the other rocks. It was black and ragged, and shaped like a witch's hat. And there was a big rock pool in front of it – but not the sort anyone would wish to paddle in. The water was dark and full of slimy seaweed.

The children could see from where they were standing that Stargazer was full of little nooks and crannies. The treasure could be hidden in any one of them.

They scrambled up on to the boulders, and started exploring round the bottom of the rock. They searched and searched, digging their hands into each little groove – but all they found was an old golf ball.

Then Arthur climbed a little way up the rock, hanging on by the juts and grooves, and poked about in the caves higher up. The smallest cave was the size of a jam jar, and the largest was as big as a hamper. To a mouse, they would have seemed quite spacious. But they did not take Arthur long to explore. He groped his hands around each cave in turn – but there was no treasure.

Soon the whole morning was gone.

'Come on,' Lucy said eventually. 'We'd better get back – it's nearly lunch time.'

'The treasure must be hidden in one of those little caves right at the top,' Arthur said, jumping back down.

Lucy frowned. 'Then how will we reach it?' she said.

'Look! I can climb up on to that,' Arthur said, pointing to a place where the rock bulged to form a small platform. 'Then I'll be able to reach across.'

'All right,' Lucy said. 'Let's come back this afternoon and try.'

Arthur tucked the map into his pocket, then they ran back to the cottage.

Mrs Blythe opened the door. She was holding a pair of oven gloves, and her face was red from cooking. 'Goodness, look at the state of you!' she exclaimed, seeing Arthur's blackened hands. 'You'll need a good wash before lunch. Whatever have you been doing?'

'We were just playing around the rock pool,' Lucy said guiltily, remembering that they had promised not to climb on the rocks.

But Mrs Blythe did not seem very interested.

'Hurry up, dears. Lunch is ready,' she said, bustling back into the kitchen. The children ran to the bathroom to wash.

'Don't let Uncle Jeremy see the map!' Lucy whispered.

'Of course I won't,' Arthur said, patting his pocket. 'I'm not that stupid!'

But unbeknown to him, there was danger lurking.

As the children walked into the dining room, General Marchmouse – dressed in his green summer uniform – was hiding under the sideboard, following their every move.

He watched as Arthur sat down in the chair

nearest him, and he saw him reach a hand into his pocket to check the map was still there.

Aha! the General thought.

He waited until Mrs Blythe had gone back to the kitchen. Then he sprang out from his hiding place, and shot up Arthur's leg like a bullet.

Arthur felt something tickling him, and darted a hand to his pocket – but the General had already snatched the map in his paws, and leapt to the floor.

Uncle Jeremy, who was sitting at the opposite side of the table, was suddenly aware of something flashing across the carpet towards the door.

He put down his fork and frowned. It looked like a mouse. In fact, he could have sworn it was a mouse. But it was *green*!

He assumed his eyes must be playing tricks on him – and he took off his spectacles and gave them a good polish.

The General moved so fast that the children, who were facing the other way, did not see him at all.

But Arthur was rummaging in his pocket. Then he turned to Lucy, looking very pale.

'The map!' he whispered. '*It's gone!*'

Chapter Five

It was only when lunch was over and they had run back upstairs to their bedroom that Arthur was able to tell Lucy what had happened.

'I felt something tickling my leg, then when I looked in my pocket, the map wasn't there!' he said. 'Something took it!'

'But what?' Lucy said. 'It must have been something very small.'

Arthur shuddered. 'It felt like a spider,' he said. 'It moved very fast, that's for sure. And it obviously knew what it was looking for – it went straight for my pocket, then shot off like a bullet!'

'A spider? But that's impossible,' Lucy replied. 'Spiders can't read maps!'

Arthur shrugged. 'Maybe it was a mouse, then.'

Lucy shook her head in bewilderment: 'But mice can't read maps either.'

The children felt very confused. Someone had taken the map, that was for sure. But whoever could it have been?

'We'd better write Nutmeg a letter, warning her the map's been stolen,' Arthur said. 'If there's someone else after the treasure, then she might know who they are.'

Lucy agreed, so they found a piece of paper, and wrote a hurried note:

Dear Nutmeg,

Arthur was looking after the map while we were having lunch, but then something ran up his leg, and dived into his pocket and stole it. He didn't see what it was, but it felt like a mouse. And now they might be looking for the treasure too. But we'll make jolly sure we find it first.

Love,

Arthur and Lucy.

They folded the letter in half and propped it against the lamp on Lucy's bedside table, where they had found Nutmeg's letter that morning.

'She'll know what to do,' Lucy said, feeling reassured.

'I hope so,' Arthur said. 'But now let's go back to the beach and start looking again. We've still got a lot of caves to explore.'

They ran downstairs. But Uncle Jeremy was waiting for them in the hall. 'How would you like to come fishing?' he asked brightly. He was holding some rods, and a canvas bag stuffed with tins and reels.

The children flinched. Normally they would have loved to go fishing. But this afternoon they had treasure to find.

'Come on, jump in the car,' Uncle Jeremy said, grabbing his straw hat. 'We might catch something for supper.'

'We'll have to go with him,' Lucy whispered, fearing Uncle Jeremy would be hurt if they refused.

'But what if someone else finds the treasure while we're gone?' Arthur asked.

'They won't,' Lucy said firmly. 'We'll only be away a few hours. No one's going to find the cave as quickly as all that.'

But unbeknown to the children, General Marchmouse had already set off. And now he was clambering down the steps to the beach, with the map clutched tight in his paw.

'I shall find the teeth first! And just let anyone stop me!' he muttered.

He jumped off the bottom step into the sand, and stared about him in astonishment. He had never been on a beach before, and it was a thrilling sight. There were huge strands of seaweed, coiled like snakes, and exotic shells coloured pink and blue and green. And there was ridge after ridge of golden sand, stretching as far as the eye could see.

The beach may have seemed small to Arthur and Lucy. But to General Marchmouse it was like a desert.

He took out his map, and noted in which direction the rocks must be. And when he looked through his field glasses, he could just see them, black and hazy in the distance.

He tucked the map back into his breast pocket, and set off towards them. It was a long way, and the sun was very hot. Soon his throat felt parched, and he could feel the sweat trickling down his shirt.

On and on he tramped, until eventually a dark shadow fell on him. And when he looked up, there they were – a range of huge black mountains, towering out of the sand!

He took out the map again, trying to work out which was Stargazer.

'It must be that one!' he cried excitedly, gazing up at the biggest mountain of them all. And when he saw how steep and craggy it was, his heart soared. The General loved danger – and he was sure to find it here.

At the base of the rock there was a smooth, flat boulder, about a foot high. He climbed on to it, pulling himself up by a strand of seaweed. When he got to the top, he saw the Rock Pool – and then even the brave General Marchmouse felt a pang of fear.

It stretched before him like a vast lake, and it looked horribly cold and slimy! On the far side of the pool, he could see the opening of a small black cave. He knew it must be the Grotto that Lord Seamouse had told them about, where the Secret Tunnel began.

But how would he reach it? It was much too far to swim.

I need a boat! he thought. And he started searching around the rock for something he could use.

Then suddenly he saw an ice-cream stick stuck under a pebble. *That will make a fine surfboard!*

he thought. He tugged it free, and lowered it into the pool. Then he slithered down on to it, so that he was lying flat on his tummy, and pushed himself off from the bank.

He waited until the stick had stopped wobbling. Then he dipped his paws into the pool and started to paddle.

The water was icy cold, and he couldn't see below the surface. He didn't like it one bit, but he kept his eyes fixed on the cave, and paddled on as fast as he could.

At least there's no sign of the Crabby Crab, he thought. *Lord Seamouse was probably making that up!*

But when he was halfway across the pool, he felt a sudden tremor beneath the water, then all at once a huge pink beast reared up in front of him.

The General lay on his ice-cream stick, quivering like jelly. It was the most hideous, pinkest creature he had ever seen. It had claws like nutcrackers, and a huge pink head with monstrous pink eyes, goggling straight at him.

'The Crabby Crab!' the General trembled.

The Crabby Crab fixed him with a very crabby stare. Then it reached out a long pink claw, and grabbed him round the stomach.

'Put me down!' the General squealed. But the Crabby Crab just squeezed him tighter. The General saw his life flash before him. He thought he was going to be gobbled up in one.

The Crabby Crab was drawing him closer and closer, and its crabby mouth was gaping.

My pistol! the General thought desperately.

But he had left it at home. Then suddenly he remembered his catapult. With a thumping heart, he fished it from his pocket, and loaded it with his last humbug.

He had catapulted many a beetle before, but never a beast as big as this. He aimed it very carefully, for he knew he could not afford to miss.

TWANG! went the elastic.

Then *THWACK!* went the humbug, as it hit the Crabby Crab smack in the eye.

The beast reared backwards, giving a roar of pain. He loosened his claw, and let the General fall *Plop!* into the pool.

The General kicked furiously, gasping for air as the seaweed and the black water swirled all around him. Then he felt something clonk against his shoulder – and when he looked up he saw the ice-cream stick floating beside him. He hauled himself on to it, and started furiously thrashing back across the pool, not daring to turn around. When he reached the bank, he heaved himself out of the water. Then he raced to the edge of the rock, and slid back down the seaweed into the sand.

And then he ran and ran and ran – faster than he had ever run before.

Puff! Pant! Stumble! Wheeze!

On and on he fled until Stargazer and the Rock Pool and the Crabby Crab were all far behind him. Then finally he collapsed, panting, in the sand.

Everything was suddenly very quiet. All the General could hear was his heart going thump.

His rucksack was soaking wet, and his clothes were covered in slime.

'The map!' he yelped, fearing he had lost it. But when he felt in his pocket it was still there.

He fished it out carefully, for the paper was sodden, and held it in the breeze to dry.

It was gone teatime, and he still had a long walk home to Seaview Hollow. He felt very wretched. He was cold and hungry, and he knew Tumtum would be furious with him when he got back.

He staggered to his feet, and started trudging miserably through the sand.

But the beach seemed to go on forever.

I must be nearly there, he thought, when he had been walking for a very long time.

But there was still no sign of the steps in the wall. He looked through his field glasses, but all he could see was sand. Never-ending sand.

'Oh dear,' he said. 'I'm lost!'

Chapter Six

Tumtum and Nutmeg and Lord Seamouse had spent a pleasant day sunbathing on the drawing-room windowsill.

It was nearly four o'clock when they finally packed up their picnic hamper and made their way back to Seaview Hollow.

'I wonder why the General suddenly darted off like that, before we'd even started our picnic?'

Nutmeg said as they climbed upstairs.

'Oh, I don't know,' Tumtum said sleepily. 'He probably went off exploring. You know the General. He can never sit still.'

But Nutmeg still felt uneasy. It was unlike the General to miss lunch.

And as they were walking home across the children's bedroom floor, she noticed the letter on Lucy's beside table.

'Oh, look, Tumtum!' she said eagerly. 'Quick, let's see what it says! Perhaps they've found the treasure already!'

Lord Seamouse waited on the floor, while Tumtum and Nutmeg climbed up the bed cover and hopped on to the bedside table. They unfolded the letter under the lamp – but when they saw what it said, their faces fell.

For the Nutmouses guessed at once that it was the General who had stolen the map from Arthur's pocket.

'I should have known he's been up to no good!' Tumtum said crossly.

They dragged the letter back down to the floor. And when they told Lord Seamouse what had happened he looked very alarmed.

'I hope the General's not still out on the beach,' he said. 'The tide will be coming in soon!'

Nutmeg turned pale. 'We must go and look for him!' she cried.

'The beach is huge, we'd never find him,' Lord Seamouse said. 'And there's no point us all getting into trouble.'

Tumtum was worried too. But he agreed with Lord Seamouse that it would be foolish to go out looking for the General now.

'Just you wait, dear – he's probably on his way home already,' he said, giving Nutmeg's paw a squeeze. 'And you know how greedy he is. He's sure to be back in time for supper!'

Just then they heard a thunder of feet on the stairs. It was Arthur and Lucy, back from their fishing trip.

'Come on, quick!' Tumtum said – and they all darted under the chest of drawers.

Lord Seamouse let them back into Seaview Hollow, then they waited anxiously for the General to reappear.

But by supper time there was still no sign

of him. Nutmeg had made a cockle pie, yet somehow no one had much appetite.

They sat in an unhappy silence, listening to the tick-tock of the clock, and to the breeze whistling under the mouse-hole door. Nutmeg pulled her shawl tighter. The thought of the General all alone on the beach made her shiver. Oh, if only he would come home!

They were quite right to be worried. For General Marchmouse was having a terrible time.

He was stumbling through the sand, with no idea which way he was going.

Goodness, he was tired!

Gradually it got dark, and the moonlight started playing tricks on him. At one point, he thought he could see a strawberry ice cream in the distance. He hurried hungrily towards it – but when he got there it was just a pink shell. He trudged on a little further. Then he saw a sight that made his heart leap. Just ahead of him, parked in the sand, was a beautiful silver car. *Hooray!* he thought. *I can drive home.* But when he reached it he let out a howl of dismay. It was just a lemonade can!

Eventually, when he thought he couldn't walk another step, he saw a castle up ahead. He staggered towards it. And this time his eyes weren't deceiving him. It was quite real – and what a splendid castle it was! It had a moat and a keep and tall yellow turrets, all built out of sand.

And there was light spilling from the arrow

slits.

That's good! he thought. *There must be someone at home!*

Whoever lived here was sure to know the way back to Smugglers' Keep.

He walked across the drawbridge, which was made from a plastic spoon. Then he poked his head through the archway.

There was a camp fire burning in the corner, and a delicious smell of roasting flies. There was no chimney, so the room was full of smoke. The General couldn't see much.

'Is there anyone at home?' he called.

No reply.

'I say, it's General Marchmouse here! Is there anyone at home?' he called again, in a rather more commanding voice.

Then he heard a horrible laugh. Laughs aren't usually horrible, but this one was. It was harsh and cackling, and it cut through the air like a whip.

Then out of the smoke there appeared the nastiest-looking mouse the General had ever seen.

He was tall and grey and whippet thin, and he was dressed in a black cape and tall scarlet boots. And he had bloodshot eyes and yellow fangs. And – most unusually – purple claws.

He gave the General a long icy stare. And yet when he spoke his voice sounded as smooth as treacle.

'I am Purple Claw,' he purred. '*Doooo* come in. You're just in time for tea.'

The General didn't like the look of him one

bit. But he was so hungry, the thought of a roasted fly lured him in.

Purple Claw didn't have much furniture. There were just two pebbles to sit on, and a purple shell for a bed.

'Sit down,' Purple Claw said, pointing to one of the pebbles.

Then he took the frying pan from the fire, and tossed the General two roasted flies, keeping four for himself.

'It's very kind of you to share your supper with me,' the General said nervously.

There were no plates or cutlery, so they ate with their paws.

It was so smoky, the General could barely see Purple Claw's face. He could just hear his jaws

smacking.

'What a nice castle you have,' the General said brightly, gobbling his food. 'Have you lived here long?'

'Only a few hours,' Purple Claw drawled. 'And I shall move out after supper.'

'Why are you leaving so soon?' asked the General, who did not know that sandcastles get washed away by the tide. Purple Claw did not reply.

'What brings *you* here?' he asked instead.

'I was just taking a little stroll,' the General said cagily. Something told him that it would be best not to tell Purple Claw about the treasure.

'The beach is a very dangerous place for a *stroll*,' Purple Claw sneered.

'Well, seeing as it was such a nice day, and seeing as I'm only in Mousewall for a week, I thought a stroll would be rather pleasant,' the General said nervously.

The conversation was not going at all as conversations should, and he suddenly felt very ill at ease. He had finished his flies, so he decided to ask for directions back to Smugglers' Keep, and get straight on his way.

'If you'll excuse me, I really must be getting home, or my friends will be worrying about me,' he said, getting up from his pebble. 'Perhaps you could be kind enough to direct me back to Smugglers' Keep –'

'*Smugglers' Keep?*' Purple Claw barked, sounding very interested.

'Yes . . . er . . . that's where I'm staying, you see – with Lord Seamouse,' the General replied. 'And . . . er . . .' He knew he was saying too much. But he was so confused, he had started to babble. 'And . . . er . . . now I really must get back. Don't worry if you don't know the way, I'm sure I'll find it. At least I've still got the map –'

'*THE MAP?* What map?' Purple Claw hissed.

'Oh, just a map of the beach, nothing . . . er . . . nothing special,' the General stammered. 'Now if you'll excuse me, it really is time I went.'

He stumbled across the room, trying to find the way out. But the smoke was so thick, everything was a haze.

Then suddenly he saw Purple Claw standing just in front of him. He was smiling a fiendish smile, and his eyes were blazing.

'Give me the map,' Purple Claw said very slowly, reaching out his paw.

'*NO I SHAN'T!*' the General squealed.

'*YES – YOU – SHALL!*' Purple Claw snarled. Then all at once the General saw a pistol being pointed at him.

He heard a peal of hideous laughter, then everything went black.

Chapter Seven

The General woke up feeling very groggy. He looked around in a daze, trying to work out what had happened.

He was lying on the floor of the sandcastle, and his clothes were sodden. The fire had gone out, and there was moonlight piercing through the arrow slits.

Suddenly he remembered Purple Claw

pointing a pistol at him – and when he felt in his pocket, the map was gone.

'The rotter!' he cried. 'Just wait till I catch him!'

He tried to get up, but he could feel a sharp pain in his lungs, and his head was throbbing.

Then he noticed a funny smell. He twitched his nose, trying to identify it. But it was so strong it made his nostrils burn. And he could see clouds of green vapour wafting in the air.

The smell hit him again – and all at once, he realised what it was.

'PEPPERMINT GAS!' he yelped. 'He's sprayed me with peppermint gas!'

The General staggered to his feet, desperate to get out. He had seen peppermint gas used in the

Royal Mouse Army, and he knew it was a terrible thing.

It is a deadly weapon, which can knock a mouse out cold, and make his nose turn blue, and his whiskers crinkle. And if a mouse inhales enough of it, his stomach knots, and his kidneys twist, and his lungs sizzle . . .

So no wonder the General felt alarmed.

He stumbled through the archway, and stood outside, taking big gulps of air. Slowly, his head stopped throbbing, and he knew he had escaped in time.

Even so, he felt very wretched.

The mission had gone horribly wrong. He had hoped to return to Seaview Hollow a hero, carrying Uncle Jeremy's teeth. But instead he had lost the map. Just think how cross Tumtum and Lord Seamouse would be when they found out! And that's if he ever managed to find his way home!

He stood miserably on the drawbridge, gazing at the vast moonlit beach. He had no idea which way to go.

But then suddenly he saw a light high up in the distance – and to his relief he realised that it was the lantern in front of Smugglers' Keep. And below it, he could just make out the pale outline of the steps in the harbour wall.

Well at least I'm not lost any more. That's one good thing, he thought, as he stepped on to the drawbridge.

But then he heard a sudden roar – and all at once a jet of ice-cold water scooped him up, and

flung him back through the archway.

There was water everywhere. Black water, swirling all around him. Round and round it went, tossing and rolling him across the castle floor.

Then it suddenly gushed away again.

The General scrabbled to his feet, and ran to the arrow slit. And when he looked down the beach he saw a sight that froze the blood in his tail – a huge foaming wave, snarling towards him.

In an instant, it reared up over his head, and smashed into the castle turret. He ran blindly across the room, and stumbled outside on to the drawbridge. The castle was tumbling to the ground, and the moat was rising. And next moment the bridge was sucked from under him, and the General was plunged into the water.

He thrashed his paws frantically, but the current was battering him in all directions.

'Help!' he cried.

Then a big wave swelled up beneath him, and spat him out into the sand.

He lay there trembling. He felt too weak to move. But he could hear the next wave thundering towards him.

With a final burst of strength, he dragged himself to his feet, and staggered towards the harbour wall. Then he started frantically clambering up the big stone steps, as the sea crashed behind him.

Finally, he reached the lane. He was out of danger now. But there was still a voice in his head crying, 'Run! Run! Run!' And run he did, as fast as his trembling legs would carry him – into the cottage, and through the kitchen, and across the hall, and up the stairs . . .

He didn't stop until he reached Seaview Hollow.

The Nutmouses and Lord Seamouse were sitting in the drawing room when they heard his exhausted *Rat! Tat! Tat!* on the front door.

'He's back!' they shouted, racing into the hall.

It was long past midnight, but they had all been much too worried to go to bed. And they were so relieved to see the General again, that at first they forgot to be cross.

'You're soaking wet!' Nutmeg cried. 'Now sit down by the fire and we'll find you some nice dry clothes to wear.'

Everyone made a great fuss of him. Lord Seamouse lent him a pair of pyjamas, and Tumtum lent him a pair of slippers, and Nutmeg hung up his suit to dry, and warmed up a big slice of pie for his supper.

They could see he was half-starved. So they waited until he had finished eating before the questions began.

'Where have you been?' Tumtum asked finally.

The General scowled. Normally he loved showing off about his adventures. But he felt that what had happened today did not show him off in a very good light.

'We know you stole the map,' Tumtum said

when he didn't answer. 'Really, General, what on earth were you playing at? You must know there's no point trying to find the treasure yourself. You could never carry it all back from the cave.'

'I just wanted to find Uncle Jeremy's teeth,' the General replied sulkily. 'The children can go and get all the rest. But *I* want to find the famous missing teeth, and bring them home all by myself, and get my picture in *The Mouse Times*. And I jolly well shall! So there!'

'Oh, no you won't!' Tumtum retorted. 'We shall return the map to Lucy's bedside table tonight. This is their treasure hunt, and you've no right to interfere!'

The General crossed his arms grumpily.

Everyone thought he was being very silly.

'We might as well take the map back now, then we can all go to bed,' Nutmeg said.

'Good idea,' Tumtum agreed, getting up from his chair. 'Come on then, General – give it back.'

The General squirmed and turned very red.

There was a tense silence. Everyone was thinking the same thing.

'You didn't . . . You didn't *lose it*, did you?' Lord Seamouse asked eventually.

The General grunted.

'Oh, how could you be such a fool?' Tumtum cried. 'You knew it was the only copy in the whole world!'

'Oh, leave me alone. I didn't lose it!' the General shouted. 'IT WAS STOLEN!'

'*Stolen?*' Lord Seamouse gulped.

'Yes, STOLEN!' the General said indignantly. 'I met a horrid villain on the beach, who lured me into his beastly sandcastle, then poisoned me with peppermint gas, then stole the map while I was out for the count! But just you wait. I'll teach that rascal to mess with *me*!'

Lord Seamouse had started to quake.

'Wh . . . wh . . . what was his name?' he stammered.

'Purple Claw,' the General replied. 'Very silly name if you ask me – silly name for a –'

But then there was a loud crash. It was Lord Seamouse, fainting on the floor.

Chapter Eight

L ord Seamouse was soon revived with a cold
flannel and a glass of port.

But he was in a terrible state.

'Purple Claw! Oh me, oh my! Oh no, oh no!'
he kept saying.

Everyone tried to calm him, but he wasn't
making any sense.

Tumtum and Nutmeg wondered who Purple

Claw could possibly be, that his name had such a terrible effect.

'Was he very frightening?' they asked the General.

'*I* certainly wasn't frightened of him,' the General lied. 'I don't know what Lord Seamouse is making such a fuss about.'

'Oh, but you don't know anything!' Lord Seamouse spluttered. 'Purple Claw is the biggest villain in all of Mousewall. Everyone trembles when they hear his name! He lurks in sandcastles, ambushing any mouse who comes near. He jumps out and says, "BOO!" and steals your picnic hamper and your fishing nets. He'll even steal your swimming trunks, if he likes the look of them! And, oh, woe betide if you make an enemy of him! He'll appear at your mouse-hole in the middle of the night, and drag you from your bed, kicking and shrieking . . . then he'll take you to the beach, and throw you to the sea horses!'

'What a horrid-sounding fellow,' Tumtum said. Nutmeg was so alarmed that as a precaution she went and bolted the front door.

'I've seen him lurking around in Uncle Jeremy's garden, watching me come and go,' Lord Seamouse quivered. 'He must have suspected that I knew where the teeth were hidden. He'd give his front fangs for them. He knows how much gold he'd get from the tooth fairies for a full set of milk teeth! If he got his claws on them he'd become so rich there would be no end to his powers. He'd build himself castles and battleships, and he'd employ his own private army to rob and steal for him, and every mouse in Mousewall would live in dread.'

'Then we must make sure the children find the treasure first!' Nutmeg cried.

'But we can't stop Purple Claw now!' Lord Seamouse trembled. 'Why, if he finds out we've been plotting against him, he'll . . . he'll . . .'

'Oh, stuff and nonsense!' the General said sharply, wishing Lord Seamouse would be a little more brave. 'We can't let that old tramp frighten us off. Besides, he'll never be able to get across the Rock Pool without a boat.'

'Oh, Purple Claw can get anywhere,' Lord Seamouse replied. 'He's got SPECIAL POWERS!'

'Well he's still only a mouse. He'll be no

match for Arthur and Lucy,' Nutmeg said firmly. 'They'll scare him off all right.'

Lord Seamouse looked a little reassured by this. He supposed even Purple Claw might be frightened when he saw the size of *them*.

'I shall write the children a letter, asking them to go back to Stargazer first thing in the morning,' Nutmeg said. 'They already know which rock the treasure's hidden in, so they shouldn't need the map.'

'But what if they can't find the right cave?' Tumtum asked. 'They've already spent a whole morning looking for it. And Stargazer's huge – it must contain a thousand nooks and crannies.'

'Tell them to search near the peak,' Lord Seamouse said. 'Whoever stole the treasure's sure to have hidden it as high up in the rock as possible. When the tide comes in the caves lower down the rock face are completely submerged – no mouse in his right mind would have hidden it there.'

'Good idea,' Nutmeg said. 'That should narrow down their search!'

Lord Seamouse found her a piece of paper, and she quickly scribbled the children a message, telling them exactly what to do.

'Arthur and Lucy won't let Purple Claw get the better of them!' she said.

When the children woke up next morning, they found Nutmeg's letter:

Dear Arthur and Lucy,

Your map has been stolen by a wicked villain called Purple Claw, who is determined to find the treasure before you do, and use it to make himself rich and powerful. But we must not let him! You must return to Stargazer at once, my dears, and resume your search. I am told the treasure is most likely to be hidden close to the rock's peak, where the tide cannot reach it. But careful how you go, for Purple Claw will be lurking. Try not to arouse his suspicions. Now hurry, my dears. For time is running out.

Love,

Nutmeg.

The children read it with astonishment.

'*Purple Claw*,' Arthur said quietly, thinking it a very strange name. 'Who do you think he is?'

'Well if he's anything like his name suggests, then he'll have purple claws,' Lucy replied. 'Maybe he's a rat!'

Arthur shuddered. Mice were one thing, but rats were quite another. Once a gang of them had kidnapped Nutmeg, and kept her prisoner on the farm pond. If it wasn't for Arthur and Lucy, she might never have escaped. From everything he had heard, rats were a very nasty breed.

He looked at his watch. It was nearly eight o'clock.

'Come on! Whoever Purple Claw is we'd better hurry if we're going to get there before he does,' he said. They quickly got dressed, then as soon as they had finished breakfast they ran outside.

But when they saw the beach they both

groaned. The sea was lapping against the rocks, and the pool was completely hidden.

'Well we can't look for the treasure now,' Arthur said.

'Is the tide coming in or going out?' Lucy asked.

'Uncle Jeremy will know,' Arthur said. They ran back inside to ask him.

'Let's see,' Uncle Jeremy said, looking at his watch. 'Yes, it'll be on its way out now.'

'How long till it goes down below the rocks?' the children asked impatiently.

Uncle Jeremy looked at them curiously. They had a whole week to play on the beach, so he wondered why they were in such a hurry.

'I'd give it an hour or two,' he said. 'Now

don't look so glum. The beach will still be there.'
Then he disappeared behind his newspaper again.

The children paced restlessly about the cottage, rushing to the window every five minutes to look out. It seemed as if the tide would never go out. But eventually it did.

'Come on!' Lucy said, and they rushed into the hall.

'Don't forget your rucksack,' Mrs Blythe said, appearing from the kitchen. 'I've packed a water bottle for you, and some biscuits.'

'Thank you!' Lucy said, taking the bag and tugging it on to her shoulder. Then they ran outside, and raced down to the beach. Arthur was carrying his toy speedboat. 'Why did you bring that?' Lucy asked.

'So we can pretend we're playing with it,' he replied. 'Nutmeg said we should try not to make Purple Claw suspicious. Well, if he sees us playing with our boat in the Rock Pool, he'll think we're just mucking about, instead of looking for treasure.'

'Good idea,' Lucy said – for they certainly didn't want Purple Claw getting wind of what they were up to.

When they reached the rocks, they scrambled up to the pool, and Lucy slung the rucksack on to the ground.

'According to Nutmeg the cave must be right up there,' Arthur said, pointing to the top of Stargazer.

'*Don't point*,' Lucy whispered. 'He might be

watching us!'

There was no one on the beach, and not a mouse or rat to be seen. But Lucy had an uncomfortable feeling, as though they were being followed.

She made Arthur feel anxious too.

'Come on, let's pretend we're playing with the boat,' he said. He knelt down beside the Rock Pool, and placed it on the water. Then Lucy knelt beside him, and pretended to be playing too. But she kept glancing over her shoulder. It was a horrible feeling – but whoever Purple Claw was, she felt sure he could see them.

And indeed he could. For Purple Claw was crouched behind a pebble on the far side of the pool, watching their every move. He was dressed in a black wetsuit, and he was holding his windsurfer.

Purple Claw wasn't fooled by the boat. From the moment Arthur pointed up to the rock, he guessed that the children were after the treasure too.

'Bother them!' he hissed.

He could see the Grotto on the far side of the pool, and he knew from the map that it was where he must get to. He had been about to slip into the water, and start windsurfing towards it – but then the children had appeared.

He crouched very still, watching Arthur and Lucy with gritted fangs. If he was to reach the treasure first, he would have to get rid of them. And there were all sorts of wicked thoughts whirring through his mind.

But Purple Claw was not the only mouse present.

Unbeknown to him, Tumtum and Nutmeg and Lord Seamouse and General Marchmouse were also there – hiding inside the pocket of Lucy's rucksack.

It had been Nutmeg who had insisted they come. She knew Purple Claw could be no match for the children. But she wanted to be there just in case.

But Purple Claw was so well hidden behind his pebble, the other mice hadn't spotted him.

The pocket was quite a squash. They were all standing tight together, with their heads poked over the side. The General was scouring the rocks with

his field glasses. He felt sure Purple Claw must be there somewhere. He had brought his catapult with him, and was looking forward to pelting him with an ink cartridge.

'Can you see him?' Lord Seamouse asked, not for the first time.

'No. Still no sign of him,' the General said – but then suddenly he caught sight of Arthur's boat, and he felt his heart throb.

It was a deep crimson, with a fat wooden steering wheel, and a motor as big as a matchbox.

Oh, what a golden opportunity this was!

The General had almost given up hope of finding the teeth by himself – for he didn't dare make another attempt to cross the pool. But in a boat such as that he would be quite safe. He could zoom into the Grotto so fast the Crabby Crab would hardly see him coming!

It was a heavenly plan! But he knew he must act fast.

He lowered his field glasses, and gave the others a sly look. Then he suddenly sprang out of the rucksack pocket, and started hurtling off across the rock.

'Come back! They'll see you!' Tumtum shouted.

But the General didn't care.

He made straight for the edge of the pool, where the children were sitting. Then he tore over Arthur's lap, and leapt down into the speedboat.

'What was that?' Arthur cried, looking round in astonishment.

The General flung himself on to the driver's seat, and turned the control switch to 'On'. There was a sudden *Vroom!* and the boat sped out across the water.

'Stop!' the children cried, trying to grab it back. But the speedboat was already out of reach. Faster and faster it went, its propellers thrashing through the slime.

The children watched in astonishment. And as the boat veered around to enter the cave, they saw a mouse in a green suit whooping at the wheel.

Chapter Nine

The boat sped into the Grotto. Then it gave a last *Vroom!* of its motor, and disappeared from sight.

Purple Claw, who was watching from behind his pebble, stamped his feet with rage.

He had left the General to drown in a sandcastle. However did he escape?

Purple Claw knew he must move fast, or the

General would reach the teeth first. He would have to windsurf after him at once – and it didn't matter if the children saw him!

He slunk out from his hiding place, and crept to the edge of the pool. But just as he was lowering his windsurfer into the water, he saw something moving in the slime. Then all at once the tip of a pincer appeared . . . and then out peeked a big goggling eye!

It was the Crabby Crab! And when he caught sight of the children, he sank back to the bottom of the pool. But he had given Purple Claw a terrible fright.

'Eek!' he cried, reeling backwards. He didn't dare windsurf across the pool now. Not with a pink monster lurking underwater!

But then how was he to reach the Grotto?

He needed a plan. And his eyes went black as he started plotting.

Tumtum and Nutmeg and Lord Seamouse, who were watching from the rucksack pocket, had also seen the General disappear.

And they were furious.

'How dare he!' Tumtum raged. 'He promised he wouldn't interfere again!'

'Oh, promises, promises! The General's never thought much of those,' Nutmeg groaned.

'Well we can't stop him now,' Lord Seamouse said. 'We'll just have to hope that Purple Claw doesn't follow him.'

'Oh, I do wish Arthur and Lucy would buck

up and find the treasure! Then we could all go home!' Nutmeg cried.

But the children were still standing beside the Rock Pool – staring at the little black hole into which the boat had disappeared.

'That mouse must have been Purple Claw!' Lucy said. 'Oh, we are stupid! Nutmeg warned us to look out for him – and now we've gone and let him steal our boat!'

'We must get it back!' Arthur cried.

But the only way to reach the Grotto was to wade into the pool. And the water looked so dark and slimy that neither child dared.

Besides, the entrance to the Grotto was very small – if the boat had gone in far, they would never be able to fish it out.

'Come on!' Lucy said. 'So long as we can find the cave, we'll still get to the treasure first!'

'All right,' Arthur said, scrambling to his feet. 'I'll climb up and look for it.'

He ran round the side of the pool, and started pulling himself up the rock face, until he could reach the top. He hugged the rock with one hand, and started groping about with the other.

Presently, his hand found a small opening in the rock. 'There's a cave here!' he shouted. 'This might be it!'

Lucy watched impatiently as he felt his hand around inside – but all he found was an old water bottle. He tossed it down to her in disgust. Then he felt all round the rest of the rock. But there were no more openings. And the top of the rock was covered in a thick blanket of moss.

Eventually, he gave up and jumped back down.

'Well, now we've looked everywhere,' he said glumly. 'The treasure can't be here after all.'

The children looked at the rocks in dismay. If the treasure wasn't in Stargazer, then wherever could it be?

Chapter Ten

It was pitch black in the Grotto. All the General could see was the pale beam of his torch, slipping over the walls.

He turned down his engine, and inched the boat forwards, searching for the Secret Tunnel.

The deeper he went, the colder the cave became. He shivered, and rubbed his paws on the steering wheel to keep warm. Then all of a sudden there was a pool of green light – and to his surprise he saw a lantern hanging from the wall.

Below the lantern, there was a small opening in the rock. And beside it, carved into the rock in big rough letters, was written:

THE
SECRET
TUNNEL

'Hurrah!' the General cried.

He chugged towards it, and tied his boat to a thin slither of rock jutting from the wall. Then he clambered up into the passage.

The tunnel twisted and turned, and got fatter and thinner, and colder and damper – and in places it was so steep that the General had to clamber along on all fours.

Eventually, he came to a big cave, the size of a shoebox. On the other side of the cave, there was a flight of stairs cut into the rock. He climbed up them – but when he got to the top, there was just a brick wall.

'Drat,' he said, thinking he had reached a dead end.

But just as he was about to turn back down the stairs, he noticed a thin ribbon of light on the floor.

And when he flashed his torch over the wall, he saw to his astonishment that there was a door cut into the rock. It didn't have a bell. There was just a rusty iron latch, and a bolt which had been left drawn.

He lifted the latch and gave it a push. It felt very stiff, as if it hadn't been used for a long time. And when it opened there was a flood of golden light.

The General stepped inside, and gave a loud gulp. He was in a cave lit by a chandelier, and filled with the most sumptuous treasures. There were paintings and tapestries, and silver candlesticks, and four-poster beds with feather duvets on top. And there was a big enamel bath, and a lavatory with a pink seat! And there were chests full of fancy jugs and plates, and a dining-room table with a china swan on top!

General Marchmouse was astonished — he had never seen such luxuries.

No wonder Lord Seamouse was so anxious to get everything back.

But the General wasn't interested in the furniture. It was Uncle Jeremy's teeth he had come for. He started rummaging through the chests, turning out the jugs and plates and cups and candlesticks, determined to find them.

Then he noticed a rusty sweet tin in the corner of the cave, with the words 'Fruit Pastilles' written on it. He scuttled over to it, and prised off the lid . . . and there they were — a whole set of fat white milk teeth, shining like pearls.

The General gasped. Just think how much the tooth fairies would pay for teeth such as these! It

was hardly surprising Purple Claw was so keen to get his paws on them.

But he was too late now!

The General quickly pressed the lid back on the tin, and heaved it up on to his shoulders.

He wanted to get away as quickly as possible, and show off about his amazing discovery. He couldn't wait to tell *The Mouse Times* that he had solved The Case of the Missing Teeth – when every other mouse in Mousewall had failed!

But as he was staggering to the door, he suddenly saw some bright beads of light coming from the back of the cave – and when he looked more closely he saw that there was a dark green curtain hanging there.

He put down the tin and walked over to it,

wondering what was on the other side. And when he touched the curtain, he found to his surprise that it was made of moss. It was so thick, he had to push his way through it with both paws – and when he came out on the other side he let out a cry.

For suddenly he was outside again! He was standing at the mouth of the cave, right at the top of Stargazer – and below him the rock fell away in a steep cliff. He could see the Rock Pool far below him, and the gulls wheeling in the air above.

He was so high up, he felt quite giddy.

He crouched down on all fours, for he was frightened of losing his balance. Then he took up his field glasses, and peered down the cliff. Arthur and Lucy had gone. But he wondered if Tumtum and the others had stayed behind.

He looked all around the beach, as far as he could see. But there was no sign of them. He supposed they must have gone back to Smugglers' Keep with the children.

Then he noticed a big sandcastle, just in front of the rocks, with a red flag flying from the turret. He twisted his lens to bring it into focus and then his heart gave a sudden jolt.

Purple Claw was standing in the watchtower with a telescope – peering straight at him.

Chapter Eleven

The General stumbled back through the curtain, shaken to the core. He knew Purple Claw had seen him. And now he would be lying in wait, ready to ambush him as he made his way home with the teeth.

The situation was hopeless. The General would never be able to get past him.

He paced anxiously about the cave, wondering

what to do.

Then all of a sudden he heard a rap on the door.

The General froze. It must be Purple Claw! But how could he have been so quick!

He grabbed a chair, and pressed himself against the wall, waiting to clobber him as he came in.

As the door opened, the General heard some muffled voices on the other side. *He must have accomplices*, he thought anxiously.

He tightened his grip on the chair, ready to bash the first mouse that appeared. But when he saw who it was he gave a cry of relief:

'Tumtum! Nutmeg! Lord Seamouse! What are *you* doing here?' he gasped.

There was a lot of explaining to be done. But when Tumtum and Nutmeg saw the treasure they were too astonished to speak.

Seaview Manor must have been the grandest doll's house in the world!

Lord Seamouse became quite emotional. He wandered about the cave in a delighted trance, gazing at his beloved possessions. He had feared he might never see them again. But here they all were – and everything intact! Some of the furniture looked a little dusty. But it was nothing that a good polish wouldn't put right.

'Just think!' he said tearfully. 'Soon everything will be returned to Seaview Manor, and I shall be able to move back into my old home again!'

The General looked sulky – for despite his

grand adventure, no one was making a fuss of him. 'I got here first!' he said stubbornly.

Tumtum turned to him savagely. He had been so overawed by the sight of the treasure, that for a moment he had forgotten how cross he was. But he had remembered now. 'I know you did, and I've a good mind to box your ears!' he said. 'We need Arthur and Lucy to carry this treasure back to Smugglers' Keep – we'll never get it home on our own. But then you try and mess everything up! First you steal the map, then the children's boat. You should be ashamed of yourself! But if you think you can spoil everything, you can think again. We've come to take you home!'

The General huffed. 'How did you come after me without a boat?' he asked. 'You're lucky the

Crabby Crab didn't catch you.'

'It was thanks to the crab that we got here,' Tumtum replied. 'After you went into the Grotto, we climbed out of the rucksack and came down to the pool, to see if we could call you back. Then the Crabby Crab poked his head out of the water. And the four of us got talking, and it turned out that he's not Crabby at all. Most delightful fellow, in fact. And when we explained why we were there, he told us all to hop on to his back – then he carried us to the Secret Tunnel.'

'Huh,' the General said. 'I wish he'd been as helpful with me.'

'And he said that if Purple Claw tries to cross the pool, he'll gobble him up!' Nutmeg added. 'So we don't have to worry about him following us up here.'

Tumtum frowned. He was looking at the walls of the cave. 'How will the children ever find the cave from the outside?' he asked. 'Look, it's completely enclosed!'

'No it's not,' the General replied. He walked to the back of the cave, and pulled aside a corner of the moss, so they could see outside.

Everyone was astonished. The cave was very well hidden. No wonder the children hadn't found it yet.

'Keep still,' the General warned them. 'When I went out earlier, Purple Claw saw me. He was lurking about in that sandcastle down there.'

'Blow,' Tumtum said. 'I hope he doesn't give us any trouble on the way home.'

'It's all right, I know another way we can go,' Lord Seamouse said. 'We can cut up beside the rocks, then creep along the bottom of the harbour wall. That way we won't have to pass the sandcastle.'

'Good,' Tumtum said. 'Now come on, we'd better get going. We've still got a long walk home.'

They all made for the door – except the General, who was hovering by the tin of teeth.

The children could fetch the rest of the treasure – but he didn't see why he should leave the teeth behind. He could carry them home himself, they weren't too heavy. Then he could tell *The Mouse Times* that it was him who had found them, and imagine what a fuss there would be!

'Come on, General – hurry up,' Tumtum said

impatiently.

'I'm bringing these with me!' the General said stubbornly, hoisting the tin on to his back.

'Don't be an ass,' Tumtum said. 'If Purple Claw sees us carrying a treasure chest across the beach, he's sure to come and ambush us!'

'Oh, bother Purple Claw!' the General snapped.

It was blowing up into quite a row. But then all of a sudden there was a huge roar outside the cave.

'It's a bird!' Nutmeg cried.

'That's not a bird,' the General said. '*That's a plane!*'

'Duck!' Tumtum cried.

At that moment, a fierce blast of wind swept open the curtain. And as the mice looked out in horror, they saw a toy aeroplane swooping towards the cave.

They flattened themselves against the wall, for it was coming straight at them. It was so close they could see into the cockpit. And what a surprise they got! For there was Purple Claw, grinning horribly as he clung to the joystick.

Chapter Twelve

Purple Claw's plane ploughed into the cave. It landed with a ferocious bang. One of the engines exploded, and there was smoke billowing down the wings.

The plane had taken a terrible battering. Everyone wondered if Purple Claw had survived – but then the roof of the cockpit flipped open, and out he stepped.

He looked very calm, despite his crash-landing.

'How do you do?' he purred, peeling off his goggles.

'You are outnumbered, Purple Claw! Now get out of here or I'll make you sorry!' the General shouted in his most menacing voice.

He stepped forwards, baring his fists – but Purple Claw just sneered. Then he reached into his cape, and whipped out his peppermint gun.

'Face the wall, with your paws behind your backs!' he barked.

And they all did, including General Marchmouse – for even the bravest mouse does what he's told when someone's pointing a peppermint gun at him.

Then Purple Claw tied them up with cotton, pulling it so tight it burned their skin.

'You rogue! You won't get away with this!' the General fumed.

'Oh yes I will!' Purple Claw said, giving him a clout. When all the prisoners were bound, he started upturning the chests and cupboards, searching for the teeth. And when he finally found the sweet tin, and prised open the lid, his heart gave a surge.

'Ha! Ha! Just think how much gold the tooth fairies will give me for all of these!' he cried. 'Oh, what a rich and powerful villain I shall be!'

In his mind's eye, he saw the life he would lead – a life of banquets, and fine clothes, and feather beds. 'I'll buy a yacht!' he shrieked, clapping his paws in delight. 'And I'll build myself a palace in the dunes, and I'll employ an army of field mice to do all my robbing and thieving!'

The idea was so glorious, it made him shiver. But this was no time for dreaming. He knew he must get out fast, in case those tiresome children came back.

He stuffed his gun back into his holster, and heaved the tin on to his shoulders.

'Cheerio, my dears!' he said mockingly – then he staggered through the door, and slammed it shut behind him.

A moment later, the mice heard the bolts being clicked shut on the other side.

'He's locked us in!' the General fumed.

They were trapped!

'Come on, let's get these ropes off. We can't do anything with our paws tied,' Tumtum said. But Purple Claw had secured the knots very tightly.

'I'll try and gnaw through them,' Nutmeg said. She leant down, and started nibbling at Tumtum's ropes.

Nibble! Nibble! Nibble!

Chomp! Chomp! Chomp!

On and on she gnawed, until her jaws ached.

The others watched tensely. Eventually, Tumtum's ropes fell free.

The others cheered. Then Tumtum quickly undid their paws too. They all rubbed their wrists, for the cotton had left red weals on their skin.

'Come on! let's try and smash open the door,' the General cried. 'Purple Claw will still be in the tunnel – we can catch him up, and spring on him from behind!'

Everyone agreed that the scoundrel must be stopped.

But though they all kicked and battered the door together, and rammed it with a chest of drawers, it wouldn't budge.

'We'll never escape!' Nutmeg said tearfully.

They felt helpless. With every second that passed, Purple Claw would be creeping further down the Secret Tunnel towards Arthur's boat.

'We must stop him!' the General cried.

Everyone wracked their brains, wondering what to do.

'I wish we could get a message to the children,' Tumtum said. 'Then we could tell them to come

back to the Rock Pool, and catch Purple Claw red-handed when he comes out of the Grotto!'

'Oh, that would serve him right!' the General said.

It was a wonderful idea. But of course it would never work, for how could they get a message to the children when they were stuck up here in the cave?

'If only Purple Claw's plane weren't smashed to bits, then one of us could fly back to Smugglers' Keep!' Nutmeg said.

The General gave a start. He had been so busy battering the door, he hadn't thought about the plane.

He turned and looked at it very carefully. Was it *really* as badly damaged as all that?

It was still belching smoke, and the wings were dented. But the propellers had survived, and the cockpit looked intact. He peered inside, and saw that the fuel gauge was showing half-full.

The General's whiskers started to quiver. 'She'll fly for me!' he said.

Chapter Thirteen

The Nutmouses and Lord Seamouse were still standing by the door, discussing what to do.

'I say, where's the General?' Tumtum asked suddenly.

Then all at once there was a deafening roar. And when they looked round they saw the aeroplane tearing across the cave, with General Marchmouse shrieking in the cockpit. There was smoke choking the wings, and the engine was spluttering.

Everyone ran for cover.

'*BRAKE!*' Tumtum shouted.

'*STOP!*' Nutmeg screeched.

But there was no stopping him now.

'Clear the Skies!' the General cried. 'I'm taking off!' Then he tore into the curtain.

Everything went black as the moss slapped over the windscreen. Then the plane slipped over the edge of the cave, and plunged into the air.

'I'm flying!' the General shouted, giggling with glee.

But when he looked out of the window he gave a loud yelp. He wasn't flying. He was sinking like a stone! And all he could see were vast black rocks, spinning all around him.

He turned to the control panel, and started yanking the knobs. But the plane kept falling.

'Help!' he cried.

He saw a green lever beside the joystick, labelled 'THROTTLE'.

He grabbed it with both paws, and wrenched it towards him.

There was a violent judder, and he felt his seat vibrate. Then the engine went '*VROOOOOM!*' and all at once the nose of the plane flipped up, and the craft soared skywards.

The General gave a whoop. He was going higher and higher, wheeling through the air like a gull.

'I am Lord of the Skies!' he cried, thumping his paw on the roof.

When he looked down, he could see Tumtum and Nutmeg and Lord Seamouse, watching him in terror from the mouth of the cave.

And how he showed off!

He looped the loop, and he did a figure of eight, then a figure of nine . . .

But then suddenly he saw an enormous shape looming towards him. It had white wings, and an orange nose.

The General gulped. It was a seagull, coming straight at him!

He yanked the joystick, trying to steer out of its path. But it was too late . . . and a moment later the bird thwacked into the cockpit.

The plane batted backwards like a cricket ball and started plummeting from the sky.

The General peered through the window in terror.

He could see the beach below him, spinning nearer and nearer . . . then there was a sudden *Smack! Bang!* as the plane crashed into a sandcastle.

The General lay in the cockpit, too dazed to move. Everything was swimming. All he could see were stars.

Then he smelt burning. 'Fire!' he cried.

He wrenched open the door, and dragged himself out. Then he started racing frantically through the sand. He saw a shell in front of him, and ducked behind it. And next moment there was a huge blast, as the plane exploded in a torrent of flames.

The General cowered there a moment, feeling

very shaken. He fished a handkerchief from his pocket, and wiped his brow. What an adventurous day it had been! And it wasn't over yet.

He still had to get a message to the children. And if they were to come back in time to catch Purple Claw, then he hadn't a moment to lose.

He dragged himself to his feet, and stumbled on through the sand. Then he clambered up the steps, shot across the lane, and wriggled into Smugglers' Keep under the garden door.

He crept through the kitchen, into the hall. He could hear voices coming from the dining room, and when he peeked round the door, he saw Arthur and Lucy sitting at the table, finishing their lunch.

He quickly searched round the hall for something to write on. Then he saw a small table against the far wall, with a telephone cord dangling down to the floor. He scrambled up it, and when he reached the table top he found a pad of white paper, and a jar of pens.

He pushed the jar over, then he pulled out a biro, and wrestled off the lid. He tore a piece of paper from the pad and, holding the pen with both arms, he scrawled out his orders:

FAO: Arthur and Lucy Mildew

Your uncle's childhood teeth have been stolen by Purple Claw, and he intends to sell them to the tooth fairies, and make himself rich and powerful. But if you do exactly as I say, you can stop him. You must proceed at once to the Rock Pool, and wait

for Purple Claw to emerge from the cave in your
speedboat. As soon as you see the boat coming, swoop
down and grab it. Then the teeth shall be yours! As
for Purple Claw — he will be yours too. Do what
you wish with him. A cage with thick bars might be
the best answer.

Yours,

General Marchmouse.

When he had finished writing, the General folded the note in half, and clenched it beneath his teeth. Then he scrambled down to the floor, and crept into the dining room.

Mrs Blythe had appeared now, and was standing beside Lucy, spooning a second helping of rice pudding into her bowl.

The General was in such a hurry, he did not even wait until she had gone. He shot straight across the carpet, and scrambled up the tablecloth. Then he leapt over the sugar dish, and dropped his letter beside Lucy's bowl.

Mrs Blythe shrieked, and dropped her spoon with a clang.

'It's that green mouse again!' Arthur cried, as the General darted back to the floor. Arthur leapt from his chair, trying to see where he went. But the General was gone.

Chapter Fourteen

Mrs Blythe shrieked and squawked and made a terrible fuss.

Uncle Jeremy had been in the drawing room, answering a telephone call. When he heard the noise he came running through.

'What's going on?' he asked.

'It was a mouse!' she cried. 'A mouse wearing *clothes*!'

'Don't be silly, Mrs Blythe. Mice don't wear clothes,' Uncle Jeremy said.

'Well, I'm telling you, this one did!' Mrs Blythe replied. 'Ask the children. They saw it!'

'Did you?' Uncle Jeremy asked, looking somewhat bewildered.

Arthur and Lucy went red. They *had* seen it – and now Lucy was clutching the General's note in her hand. But they didn't want to have to start explaining everything to the grown-ups.

'There was a mouse,' Lucy said. 'It ran across the table. Then it ran off again.'

'And was it wearing clothes?' Uncle Jeremy asked, clearly thinking this all very silly.

'I . . .er . . . I didn't notice,' Lucy mumbled.

'Nor did I,' Arthur said.

'But it *was*,' Mrs Blythe cried. 'I tell you, it *was*!'

Uncle Jeremy gave Mrs Blythe a kindly look. He wondered if it was the hot weather that had made her so muddled.

'Well I can assure you, if I see it I'll send it running!' he said. But Mrs Blythe did not look at all reassured.

As soon as lunch was finished, Arthur and Lucy ran upstairs to read their letter. The General's writing was much bigger than Nutmeg's, so they did not need a magnifying glass. Arthur sat next to Lucy on the bed, while she read it out loud.

'So there we were thinking the mouse in the green suit was Purple Claw – but he's on *our*

174

side,' Arthur said.

'And he's a General!' Lucy said in astonishment.

The children had never heard of the Royal Mouse Army, so they hadn't known that mice could be Generals.

'Do you think Purple Claw is a mouse too?' Arthur asked – for the General's letter hadn't made it clear.

'He must be, if he's small enough to fit in the boat,' Lucy said.

'Come on!' Arthur said, jumping up from the bed. 'Whoever he is we'd better go and catch him!'

'We'll need something to put him in,' Lucy said. 'We should take a biscuit tin.'

'We needn't bother. We can put him in a fishing net,' Arthur said.

'All right,' Lucy agreed. So they ran downstairs and grabbed their fishing nets from the hall, then they raced back to the beach.

Tumtum and Nutmeg and Lord Seamouse, meanwhile, were looking out anxiously from the mouth of the cave.

They had seen the General's plane crash into the sandcastle. And they had seen him clamber out of the wreckage, and start scurrying back towards Smugglers' Keep.

And when they saw Arthur and Lucy charging back across the sand, they knew he must have got his message to them, and warned them what was going on.

'Oh, hooray. They're back!' Nutmeg cried.

'And look! They've brought nets to catch Purple Claw!' Lord Seamouse said gleefully.

They couldn't wait to see what happened.

'Hurry, hurry!' they all cried, fearing the children might not reach the pool in time.

The mice watched as Arthur and Lucy scrambled up on to the rocks, and stood waiting by the pool with their nets.

But they waited and waited – and still Purple Claw didn't come. The Rock Pool was quite still. There was nothing stirring, not even a dragonfly.

'Do you think he's escaped already?' Lucy asked.

'He can't have done, otherwise the boat would be here,' Arthur said.

The mice craned over the ledge, trying to see what was going on. It seemed like ages since Purple Claw had left the cave. He should have reached the Grotto by now, and found the boat. They wondered why he was taking so long.

Then suddenly Tumtum noticed Lucy looking their way.

'Keep still!' he hissed.

But it was too late. Lucy had seen them moving out of the corner of her eye, and now she was staring straight at them.

'Look!' she cried. Then Arthur saw them too – three little mice high up on the rock, dressed in smart summer clothes! The children stared at them in astonishment.

'However did they get up there?' Lucy said.

'They must have come out from behind that green plant,' Arthur replied. 'Maybe that's where the cave is. I'm going to have a look.'

'Oh, do be careful,' Lucy said. 'They might bite!'

But Arthur was already scrabbling up the rock.

'Quick, get inside!' Tumtum said. And the mice all ran back through the curtain, into the cave.

Arthur pulled himself up slowly, gripping the rock with both hands. When he was about a metre off the ground he found a little grove to tuck his feet into. He hugged one arm around the rock to keep his balance. Then he reached out his other arm, and pushed his hand into the moss.

It was thick and slimy. But when he pressed his hand all the way through, he could feel a hole on the other side.

'There's a cave here all right!' he shouted down to Lucy.

'Is there anything in it?' she asked excitedly.

'Hang on,' he said, pushing his hand in deeper.

He stretched out his fingers, and groped them round the floor.

Tumtum and Nutmeg and Lord Seamouse pressed themselves against the wall, watching in terror as the huge, pink hand came closer and closer.

'Quick! Let's hide over there in the wardrobe!' Tumtum whispered.

They jumped over Arthur's thumb, and ran towards it. They all squeezed in together, then Tumtum pulled the doors tight shut.

'Shhh!' he whispered. 'Keep very still!'

Arthur pushed his hand deeper into the cave. Then suddenly his fingers bumped into something solid. It felt like wood. He grabbed it in his fist, and pulled it out.

'It's a wardrobe!' he cried.

'Let's see!' Lucy said.

He passed it down to her, and she looked at it in astonishment. It was the prettiest piece of doll's house furniture she had ever seen. The wood was painted pale blue, and the knobs were made of tiny pearls.

It felt very heavy. *I wonder if there's anything*

inside, she thought. She tried to pull the door open, but it was stuck – Tumtum had locked it from the inside.

Arthur turned and reached back into the cave.

'There's masses more!' he said excitedly, fishing out a four-poster bed.

Lucy put the wardrobe on the ground. And as she reached up to take the bed from Arthur, the door squeaked open, and Lord Seamouse and Tumtum and Nutmeg crept out.

'Come on! Let's hide here,' Tumtum said, leading them behind a fat grey pebble.

They crouched behind it, watching as Arthur pulled more and more treasures from the cave.

'Here's a bath . . . and a piano . . . And look!

There's even a ping-pong table!' he cried.

He passed each item down to Lucy, who packed them into her fishing net. She could hardly wait to take everything back to Seaview Manor. Just think how grand it would look!

'That's the lot,' Arthur said eventually, when he had explored the last inch of the cave.

'What about the mice?' Lucy asked. 'I wonder where they disappeared to.'

'They must have got out somehow. I bet the rock's full of secret tunnels,' Arthur said.

He clambered down, then the children stood by the Rock Pool, admiring all the lovely things they had found.

But there was still no sign of the boat.

'Where can it be?' Arthur said.

'*Shhh!*' Lucy said suddenly. 'What's that?'

The children both crouched by the pool and listened. They could hear a rumbling noise, coming from somewhere deep inside the rock. It was only faint at first. But then it got louder and louder, until it became a *Vroom! Vroom! Vroom!*

'It's the boat! He's coming!' Arthur whispered. He grabbed his fishing net, then they both waited by the pool, keeping very still.

'He won't get past *us*!' Lucy said.

Chapter Fifteen

Purple Claw shivered with glee — for his job was almost done.

He had trudged all the way down the Secret Tunnel, lugging the tin of teeth on his shoulders. The tin was very heavy, and it had been a terrible slog. So imagine his joy when he finally reached the Grotto, and found the speedboat tied to the wall.

He heaved the tin down into the boat, then he

jumped in and undid the mooring rope.

He flashed his torch over the control panel, and pressed the knob marked 'On'. The engine spluttered, then the boat slowly pulled out on to the water. Purple Claw chugged forwards, until he could see the big arch of sunlight at the mouth of the Grotto.

He pointed the boat towards it. Then he tightened his grip on the steering wheel, and slammed his paw on the accelerator.

The engine roared. The propeller span. Then the boat reared up its nose, and shot forwards like a bullet.

'No one can stop me now!' Purple Claw cried as he sped into the sunlight.

The boat skimmed across the Rock Pool –

Buong! Buong! Buong! – with seaweed splattering the windscreen.

'The teeth are mine!' Purple Claw shrieked. '*Mine! Mine! Mine!*'

Then suddenly a black shadow fell over him. And next thing the boat flew into the air.

Purple Claw frantically wrenched the steering wheel – left! right! left! – thinking he had been biffed by a wave. But the boat kept rising.

He stood up, and peered out over the windscreen. Then he let out a terrible squeal.

He was caught in a fishing net!

'Help!' he cried, as Arthur and Lucy gazed at him in astonishment. They thought he looked very odd.

And it wasn't just his long black cape, or his

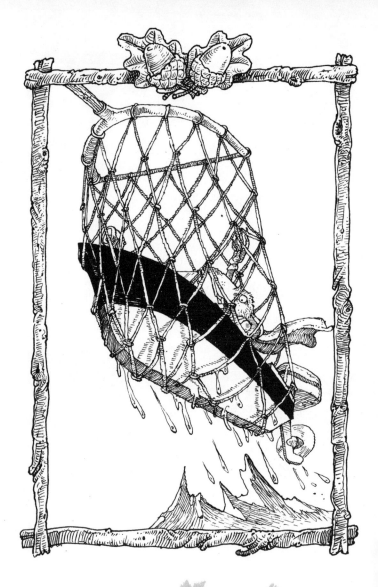

scarlet boots or his purple claws that were so unusual. He was simply the mangiest, meanest, most horrible-looking mouse they had ever seen.

'Are Uncle Jeremy's teeth in there?' Lucy said, peering into the net.

'They must be in that sweet tin,' Arthur replied.

But Purple Claw looked so nasty, neither child dared reach down a hand to take it out.

Tumtum and Nutmeg and Lord Seamouse watched in delight from behind the pebble.

'What will they do with him?' they all asked. The children were wondering just the same thing.

He didn't look the sort of mouse one would wish to keep as a pet. And yet he was a villain, so now they had caught him, they couldn't just let him go.

'Let's take him back to Smugglers' Keep, and tip him out into the bath,' Arthur suggested.

'All right,' Lucy said. 'Uncle Jeremy will know what to do with him. Now that we've found the treasure, we can tell him the whole story.'

They hurried back across the beach.

Lucy carried the fishing net full of the doll's house furniture, and Arthur carried the net containing Purple Claw, who squealed and scrabbled all the way home.

Tumtum and Nutmeg and Lord Seamouse followed them. But they couldn't run as fast as the children, so they trailed some way behind.

When the children got back to Smugglers' Keep, Mrs Blythe let them in.

'What have you caught in there?' she asked Arthur, seeing the net swinging back and forth on the end of his rod.

'Er, nothing . . .' Arthur mumbled, edging past her.

The children didn't want Mrs Blythe to see Purple Claw, or she would be sure to start shrieking again.

'Just something we fished out of the Rock Pool,' Lucy explained hurriedly. Then they fled upstairs before she could ask any more questions.

They ran into the bathroom, and locked themselves in. Then Arthur shook the fishing net over the bath, and Purple Claw and the boat and the sweet tin all tipped out.

Purple Claw tore up and down, trying to

escape. But the bath was very deep, and he couldn't get out.

He saw Arthur and Lucy peering down at him, and shook his fists with rage:

'You hateful little creatures!' he cried. 'I'll get my revenge for this! Just you wait and see!' But all the children heard was a squeal.

When Purple Claw was at the other end of the bath, Lucy quickly reached down and picked up the tin.

Purple Claw gave a howl, and rushed towards her, gnashing his fangs.

But the bath was so slippery, he skidded over and landed flat on his back, kicking his scarlet boots in the air.

Lucy prised off the lid of the tin, and the

children looked inside. And there they were, Uncle Jeremy's milk teeth! It was strange to see them.

'They must be ancient,' Arthur said. 'Nearly as old as he is!'

'We'd better give them back to him,' Lucy said.

Arthur agreed, so they put the lid back on the tin, then they left Purple Claw alone in the bath and went downstairs.

Uncle Jeremy was in the drawing room, reading a book about fishing. He could see from the children's faces that something very serious had taken place.

And when they showed him the tin of teeth, and told him that they all belonged to him, from when he was a little boy, he was very surprised.

He had given his teeth to the tooth fairies. He hadn't expected to see them again.

'Wherever did you find them?' he said.

So the children told him the whole story, beginning with the map on the bedside table, and ending with Purple Claw's dramatic capture on the Rock Pool.

The only thing they left out was Nutmeg, for she had warned them ages ago that they must never tell anyone about her. But after she had left the map on the bedside table, she didn't come into the story much. So they managed not to mention her.

Uncle Jeremy listened very carefully. He didn't interrupt, and he didn't make them feel silly, as some grown-ups might have done.

'So what did you do with Purple Claw?'

he asked.

'He's upstairs in the bath!' Lucy said. 'Come and have a look at him. He's the strangest mouse you've ever seen.'

Uncle Jeremy didn't really believe that the children had found a mouse with purple claws of course. But he didn't want to spoil their fun. So he levered himself out of his chair, and followed them upstairs.

Lucy opened the bathroom door, and let him go in first. And when he saw Purple Claw he got such a fright he fell over backwards, and crashed into the towel rail.

It was just as the children had said . . . a cross, mangy little mouse, with a black cape and scarlet boots. . . and *purple claws*!

Uncle Jeremy pulled off his spectacles, and gave them a good polish. Then he stood up, and peered into the bath again.

'Astonishing. Quite astonishing. Quite, quite astonishing,' he said over and over again. He had seen mice before in Smugglers' Keep – but never one like this.

'What shall we do with him?' the children asked.

'We must treat him like a king!' Uncle Jeremy replied. 'Go down to the kitchen, and ask Mrs Blythe for the finest mouse-sized morsels she can find. Bring him cheese and chocolates and the tastiest slithers of ham!'

'What's he done to deserve that?' Arthur asked.

'Don't you see, he is a rare breed!' cried Uncle Jeremy, hopping round the room in excitement. 'He's the rarest of the rare! The strangest of the strange! We must put him in a cage, and lend him to the zoo, so that everyone can come and look at him! He shall be the most famous mouse in the whole wide world!'

Chapter Sixteen

The rest of the day passed in a daze.

Uncle Jeremy telephoned all the local newspapers, and soon the house was full of reporters and photographers jostling to see Purple Claw in the bath.

Everyone wanted to ask the children questions:

'So this mouse who appeared on the dining-room table was wearing a suit, you say?'

'And he left you a letter?'

'And he signed himself General Marchmouse?'

Somehow, the children sensed that the reporters didn't believe a word they were saying.

'They think we've made it up,' Arthur whispered, when he and Lucy finally had a moment on their own.

'But they've seen Purple Claw, so they must know it's true,' Lucy said.

'They probably think we dressed him up in doll's clothes, and painted his toes purple ourselves,' Arthur said. 'You know what grown-ups are like.'

It was true, grown-ups could be horrid. The children started wishing they would all go away.

But then suddenly one of the reporters pointed across the room, and let out a shriek.

The other reporters all turned to look. And to their astonishment they saw a little mouse marching up and down the mantelpiece, swishing a match at them.

And he was dressed in a green suit!

'Don't believe a word those children tell you!' he roared. '*I* discovered the treasure first, and if it hadn't been for me, no one would ever have found it! It was all thanks to *me*! The great General Marchmouse!'

No one could understand a word he was saying, of course – for, to the human ear, his voice was just a squeal. But the General didn't care. He strutted up and down, boasting and saluting, and

causing a terrible stir.

The reporters became very excited, and started shouting into their mobile telephones saying, 'Hold the front page!'

Everyone was egging the General on.

The General was a natural show-off, and he didn't need much encouragement. He puffed his chest and preened his whiskers, and posed beside a china shepherdess.

The children stood at the back of the room, watching with delight.

'They'll have to believe us now!' Arthur said.

The General showed off for a whole hour solid. Then one of the reporters cried, 'Come on! Let's catch him, and take him back to the office in a cardboard box!'

'Just you try!' the General roared. Then he leapt to the floor, and shot out of the door, moving so fast no one could stop him.

Tumtum and Nutmeg and Lord Seamouse had just returned from the beach. As they came inside, they heard a terrible commotion.

They crept across the kitchen floor, and peeked into the hall – just in time to see General Marchmouse fleeing from the drawing room.

'General, over here!' Tumtum cried.

The General shot towards them, then they all darted into the vegetable rack, and hid inside the leaves of a cabbage.

The reporters saw the General fleeing into the kitchen, and stormed after him.

'He must be here somewhere!' they cried,

and started turning out the cupboards. The mice trembled in the cabbage, terrified they would turn out the vegetable rack too. But when Mrs Blythe saw what a mess they were making, she shooed them away with a tea-towel.

Finally, the kitchen was quiet. But the mice were very shaken. 'Whatever's been going on?' Nutmeg whispered.

'Some reporters came to see me,' the General replied grandly. 'They tried to kidnap me – I think they wanted to make me into a television star!'

'What a terrible thought!' Tumtum shuddered.

They could still hear people clonking about in the hall. 'Let's stay here until everyone's gone,' Nutmeg said. 'We don't want to take any more chances.'

They stayed hidden inside the cabbage for a long time. They waited until the last reporter had left the house, and until they had heard Uncle Jeremy and the children going upstairs to bed. Only when everything was absolutely quiet and still did they dare to clamber out of the vegetable rack, and start creeping back to Seaview Hollow.

But as they were passing the drawing-room door, they heard someone snoring. And when they peeked inside, they saw the most astonishing sight. In the middle of the floor was a big cage, with a domed roof and gold bars. It was the most magnificent cage they had ever seen, almost like a palace.

They crept over to it, and looked through the

bars. And there was Purple Claw – and didn't he look grand! He was fast asleep in a bed of duck feathers, with a swollen stomach, and a dreamy smile on his face. Beside his bed was a pretty china trough, full of raisins and pastry crumbs, and crisps and chocolates, and slithers of the finest, smelliest cheese.

'These bars look very flimsy. I shouldn't be surprised if he doesn't manage to break out!' Lord Seamouse said anxiously.

'Oh, he shan't do that,' Tumtum said. 'Just see how fat and contented he looks. He's the luckiest villain there ever was!'

Tumtum was quite right, of course. Purple Claw had done very well for himself – much better than he deserved. Next morning, he would be taken

to the zoo, where he would live happily ever after in his gilded cage, being fêted and fussed over, and given delicious things to eat.

And he would never bother any mouse again.

Finally, the Nutmouses, the General and Lord Seamouse clambered upstairs, and crept into Arthur and Lucy's bedroom. The children were asleep, but they crossed the floor on tiptoe all the same. But when they saw the doll's house, they all let out a cheer.

For it was a splendid sight. The children had put all the furniture back in place, and arranged all the tapestries and the paintings and the lamps and the candlesticks, and replaced the bath and the basin and the lavatory. They had even made Lord

Seamouse's bed!

'Gracious,' Tumtum said enviously. 'It's even grander than Nutmouse Hall!'

When he saw all his pretty things again, Lord Seamouse shed a tear. His dark days in Seaview Hollow were over. Now he would be Lord Seamouse of Seaview Manor again!

'Come in, come in!' he said, longing to show the other mice round. He took them upstairs and downstairs, and everyone was very impressed.

'Oh, look!' Lord Seamouse cried when they came to the drawing room. For there were Uncle Jeremy's teeth, neatly arranged in the glass cabinet! How delightful to see them back on display!

And when they reached the dining room, they found that the children had left them a dish of breadcrumbs and a whole chunk of chocolate for their supper.

Lord Seamouse sliced the chocolate with his carving knife, and served everything on his best silver plates, then they all sat talking and eating late into the night.

And there we must leave them, for their adventures are over, at least for now. And Arthur and Lucy's adventures are over too. But there was so much chatter and laughter coming from the doll's house that, as the night wore on, Lucy started to toss and turn. And it was a funny thing, but as she was drifting back to sleep she could have sworn she saw someone peeking at her from the bedside table. Someone with a long, nutmeg tail.